**BOOK ANALYSIS**

Written by Angela Youngman

# The Lion, the Witch and the Wardrobe

BY C. S. LEWIS

BrightSummaries.com

# C. S. LEWIS

## BRITISH WRITER

- **Born in Belfast in 1898.**
- **Died in Oxford in 1963.**
- **Notable works**
  - *The Screwtape Letters* (1942), fictional letters
  - *The Space Trilogy* (1938-1945), science fiction
  - *Surprised by Joy* (1955), autobiography

C. S. Lewis (full name Clive Staples Lewis) was a writer, lecturer, academic, broadcaster and lay theologian. As a child he adopted the name of Jack and was known by this for the rest of his life. From an early age, he loved to read, and was influenced by Beatrix Potter's (English writer, 1866-1943) animal stories. This led him and his brother Warnie to create their own fictional world of Boxen, which was inhabited and run by animals. His later education introduced him to other literary influences such as the Icelandic sagas, Norse mythology, Greek literature and mythology. He also served as a soldier in France during World War I (1914-1918). Unhappiness at school, the loss of his mother and the horrors of wartime led him to become an atheist.

After demobilization, he returned to his studies at Oxford University, eventually teaching English Literature at Magdalen College there. Along with J. R. R. Tolkien (English writer, 1892-1973), he was a founder member of the Inklings, a literary discussion group that met at Oxford University. His friendship with Tolkien also helped to reawaken his Christian faith. His fantasy series *The Chronicles of Narnia* (1950-1956), the first of which was *The Lion, the Witch and the Wardrobe*, were written during these years in Oxford. He remained at Oxford University throughout World War II (1939-1945), where he served in the Home Guard, as well as taking part in religious broadcasts on the BBC. In 1954, he began teaching at Magdalene College, Cambridge University, but maintained a home in Oxford. In 1956, he married the American writer Joy Davidman (1915-1960). Lewis has had a deep influence on English literature, not only through his own work, but though his involvement in the Inklings, and as an academic tutor to other English writers like John Betjeman (1906-1984) and Roger Lancelyn Green

(1918-1987). His writing reflected his Christian faith, as he used fictional writing as a way of making Christian beliefs understandable to ordinary people. During his lifetime, he wrote over 30 books, many of which have been translated into more than 30 languages with stories like *The Chronicles of Narnia* selling millions of copies. His work helped to develop modern children's literature, fantasy as a genre, and subsequently influenced writers such as Tim Powers (American author, born in 1952) and J. K. Rowling (born in 1965).

# *THE LION, THE WITCH AND THE WARDROBE*

## CHILDREN'S FANTASY STORY

- **Genre:** children's fantasy
- **Reference edition:** Lewis, C. S. (1959) *The Lion, the Witch and the Wardrobe*. London: Penguin.
- **1st edition:** 1950
- **Themes:** fantasy, adventure, Christianity, good vs. evil, sin, universal morality, redemption

*The Chronicles of Narnia* are a series of books that follow the story of the world of Narnia from its creation to its end and eventual resurrection in an afterlife. Some critics have suggested that each of the seven books reflects one of the seven deadly sins, but for Lewis the aim was much simpler: to transcribe images that had flashed through his mind onto paper and spin them into a story. *The Lion, the Witch and the Wardrobe* had a long gestation period, as the image of a faun holding packages in a snowy wood had been with Lewis since he was 16 years old. Later came the images of a street lamp and a Queen on a sleigh, and he began to create a story around them, not knowing what would happen next. He wrote that one day Aslan bounded in, and the story just fell into place. As a confirmed Christian, Christian ideas and themes were an added dimension to the story. The stories were read and discussed during meetings of the Inklings.

The books were not written in chronological order. *The Lion, the Witch and the Wardrobe* was the first in the series to be written, and was published in 1950. This was followed by: *Prince Caspian* (1951), *The Voyage of the Dawn Treader* (1952), *The Silver Chair* (1953), *The Horse and His Boy* (1954), *The Magician's Nephew* (1955), and *The Last Battle* (1956).

The suggested reading order of the series (following the internal chronology of the story) is as follows:

- *The Magician's Nephew*;
- *The Lion, the Witch and the Wardrobe*;
- *The Horse and His Boy*;
- *Prince Caspian*;
- *The Voyage of the Dawn Treader*;

- *The Silver Chair*;
- *The Last Battle*.

C. S. Lewis has had a tremendous influence on children's writing, fantasy and science fiction, religious writing and academia. *The Chronicles of Narnia* have been widely translated, are published worldwide, and have been turned into films and TV programmes.

# SUMMARY

## DISCOVERY OF NARNIA

World War II is underway and the four Pevensie children – Peter, Susan, Edmund and Lucy – have been evacuated to the countryside to live with Professor Kirke. One rainy day, they play a game of hide and seek within the house. Lucy finds a large, carved wardrobe and goes inside to hide. The wardrobe is full of fur coats and she tries to hide behind them. As she moves backwards, she suddenly finds herself in a snowy woodland landscape. Curious, she goes for a walk, heading towards a light she can see in the distance. It turns out to be a lamp post permanently glowing in the forest. As she looks at it, a faun appears under it, carrying an armful of packages. The faun, whose name is Mr Tumnus, is surprised to see her, and upon discovering she is a human child, tells her she is in the land of Narnia and invites her to tea. Lucy accepts and has a nice time until Mr Tumnus begins to cry, explaining that he has done something extremely wicked.

He is a servant of the White Witch, who has ordered him to capture any human child that appears. The Witch rules Narnia, and has placed the land under an enchantment that ensures that it is always winter, and never Christmas or spring. The arrival of human children could break that spell. Lucy asks him to let her go, and he agrees because he likes her. On her return home, she tells her siblings about her adventure but they do not believe her. No time has passed in our world, and she seems to have been gone only a few seconds. They look in the wardrobe and see only a wooden back.

Edmund teases her continually. One day, seeing her go back into the wardrobe, he follows her and they both enter Narnia. Edmund meets the White Witch, who claims she is the Queen of Narnia. He tells her about Lucy's visit, and that he has two other siblings. The White Witch says that she will make him her heir, and his siblings princes and princess of his court, if he brings them all to meet her. She gives him enchanted Turkish Delight to eat and says he can only have more if he returns with his siblings. On his way back to the wardrobe, Edmund meets Lucy who is really pleased he has discovered Narnia. Lucy has been having tea again with Mr Tumnus. When they meet Peter and Susan, Edmund spitefully says that Lucy is making up stories and that there is no such thing as Narnia. Peter and Susan are worried, and seek help from Professor Kirke who uses logic to demonstrate that Lucy may be telling the truth.

The next encounter with Narnia comes when all four children are seeking to escape from the housekeeper and go to hide in the wardrobe. All four now enter Narnia. Peter and Susan are very apologetic towards Lucy, and they go to meet Mr Tumnus. They find he has been arrested because he has helped a human child - Lucy. Determined to save him, Lucy asks her siblings to help. Guided by a friendly robin, they meet Mr Beaver who takes them to his home and tells them about Aslan. Three of the Pevensies are immediately thrilled to hear Aslan's name, even though they do not know him. However, Edmund finds the name loathsome. Mr Beaver explains that Aslan is a lion, the king of the Beasts, and the son of the Emperor-over-the-Sea.

## EDMUND'S BETRAYAL

Since entering Narnia with his siblings, Edmund has been very quiet. He makes some comments that reveal that he had lied about being in Narnia on a previous occasion, which leads to a confrontation with Peter, who is angry about Edmund's spiteful treatment of Lucy. Edmund then tries, but fails, to persuade them to walk towards the witch's castle rather than go to Mr Tumnus.

Although he accompanies the others to the Beavers' house, he leaves unnoticed during the evening. He wants more Turkish Delight, and believes the Witch will make him her heir. He has a difficult journey through the snow-covered countryside, and upon entering the castle he makes fun of the stone animals he finds in the courtyard. Edmund meets Maugrim, a wolf who is chief of the White Witch's secret police, who takes him to the Witch. The Witch is angry because he has not brought his siblings, and refuses to provide him with more Turkish Delight. She becomes incandescent with rage when she discovers that Edmund's siblings are on their way to meet Aslan at the Stone Table. The wolves are sent out to capture everyone in the Beavers' cottage. Edmund is tied to her sleigh and forced to walk behind it as the Witch heads for the Stone Table. He is now her captive. As the journey progresses, it becomes evident that winter is giving way to spring at last. Eventually Edmund is tied to a tree and the Witch prepares to execute him there, rather than at the Stone Table, the traditional place of execution. She says that if at least one of the children is dead, then the ancient prophecy that four humans will overthrow her rule and reign in the castle of Cair Paravel cannot come true.

## MEETING ASLAN

Discovering that Edmund is missing, Mr and Mrs Beaver and the three remaining children search for him without success. The Beavers eventually convince Peter, Susan and Lucy that the only way to save Edmund is to seek the help of Aslan, because only Aslan has the power to deal with the Witch. They quickly gather their things and rush to meet Aslan. The Wolves arrive too late, and begin to track them across the frozen ground.

Hearing sleigh bells, the Beavers and children hide, thinking it is the Witch. They then discover it is Father Christmas - an indication that the Witch's hold on Narnia is loosening. The spell of 'Always winter, never Christmas' has ended. Father Christmas gives them gifts: Mr Beaver is told his dam has been repaired, and new sewing equipment is provided for Mrs Beaver. Peter is given a sword and shield, Susan receives a bow and arrows, as well as a magical horn, while Lucy receives a healing cordial to use when needed. Leaving Father Christmas, they continue on their way to the Stone Table where they meet Aslan and his followers.

The children are awed by the majesty of Aslan, but instinctively love him. Aslan asks where the fourth human child is. Peter explains, and apologies for his own treatment of Edmund, which has contributed to Edmund's decision to go to the Witch. Aslan promises to do all that he can to save Edmund. He takes Peter to show him Cair Paravel, the castle where he will be High King. Then they hear Susan's horn, signalling that she is in danger. Peter is sent to help her so that he can win his spurs, and finds that one of

Maugrim's wolves has attacked Susan, who has taken refuge in a tree. Peter fights and kills the wolf. Aslan knights him, giving him the name Sir Peter Wolfsbane. Meanwhile, Aslan's followers track another wolf back to the witch, and save Edmund. The Witch escapes by disguising herself as part of the landscape.

Edmund is reunited with his siblings and apologises. He has a long talk with Aslan, and begins to understand what he has done wrong. The Witch appears and demands Edmund's life because he is a traitor and the Deep Magic has given her rights over all traitors. Aslan reaches a secret compromise with her which leaves him very downcast.

## DEATH AND RESURRECTION

Aslan orders everyone to move from the Stone Table to another site. He has long conversations with Peter, giving lots of advice on how to conduct a battle with the Witch's army. That night, Aslan secretly leaves the encampment. Unable to sleep, Susan and Lucy see him go and follow him. When Aslan realizes they are there, he says that they can walk with him, and that he would appreciate the company, but that when he tells them to leave they must do so. Soon he asks them to walk beside him, with their hands in his mane giving him comfort. He appears to be deeply troubled. Near the Stone Table, Aslan turns to the children and tells them that they must go no further, and should hide until it is safe to return to their brothers. Once in hiding, the girls watch in horror as Aslan goes on alone to meet the Witch. He allows the Witch and her followers to torment him, tie him up, cut his mane and kill him on the table, and the girls realise that Aslan has taken Edmund's place as a sacrifice. After the Witch's army leaves to attack Aslan's army, Susan and Lucy go over to Aslan's dead body and mourn. Mice come and eat through his bonds. As dawn breaks, the Stone Table cracks and Aslan disappears. Then the girls hear his voice. Aslan has risen from the dead. This is the secret of the Deeper Magic: when an innocent willingly allows himself to be sacrificed for a traitor, death itself starts working backwards, thus leading to Aslan's resurrection.

## THE AFTERMATH

A joyous game of chase begins as Aslan regains his strength. Susan and Lucy ride on his back to the Witch's castle, where he breathes on the creatures she has turned to stone and frees them. They all head for the battle against the Witch's troops, arriving just in time. Peter and his army are exhausted, and many of the army have been turned to stone by the Witch's wand. Realising this, Edmund fought his way to her and destroyed her wand, but was seriously injured in the fight. Aslan attacks the Witch and kills her. Peter's army, helped by all the new arrivals, defeats the Witch's followers.

Lucy uses her healing cordial to save Edmund, as well as many other injured members of Peter's army. Aslan knights Edmund, who has now fully atoned for his sins. Everyone heads for Cair Paravel, where Aslan crowns the four children. Peter becomes the High King. The children grow up and reign in peace in Narnia during an era known as the Narnian Golden Age. They have many adventures. One day, they hear the tale of a White Stag that has appeared in the far northern reaches of Narnia. They decide to find it. During their journey, they come across a lamp post and begin to remember their previous lives in England, retracing their steps to the wardrobe. They tumble out into the room. No time has passed. They have returned as the children they were at the start of their adventures in Narnia, but with clear memories of Aslan and their adventures. Having left fur coats from the wardrobe in Narnia, they go to explain the situation to Professor Kirke. He reassures them that they will return to Narnia one day, but not by the same route, hinting that he himself has been there, and tells them that "Once a king or queen in Narnia, always a King or Queen in Narnia" (p. 170).

# CHARACTER STUDY

## ASLAN

Aslan is the sovereign ruler of Narnia, the son of the Emperor-over-the-Sea. He has many realms, and appears as a Lion – the king of the beasts – in Narnia, because Narnia is a land where animals talk. When his name is mentioned, people either love or are immediately horrified by it. Peter, Susan and Lucy are delighted by it, while Edmund, who has come under the influence of the White Witch, hates the sound of the name. Aslan has immense power but he gives people the freedom to make their own choices. His arrival in Narnia marks a time of change, and he sets wrongs to rights. He is noble, awe-inspiring and a little frightening, full of complete goodness and love for everyone within his care. He willingly sacrifices his life for Edmund. While he knows of the magic beneath the Deep Magic, he can only trust and believe that the resurrection will happen, as it has not been tested in this way before.

Aslan does not stay in one country, as Mr Beaver explains:

> "He'll be coming and going. One day you'll see him and another you won't. He doesn't like being tied down – and of course, he has other countries to attend to. He'll often drop in. Only you mustn't press him. He's wild, you know. Not a tame lion." (p. 165)

Aslan is the allegorical equivalent of Jesus Christ. The death and resurrection scene is a metaphor for the crucifixion and resurrection of Jesus. Susan and Lucy keep him company on his last walk to the Stone Table. Even though he knows that a greater magic exists, he is still unhappy and reluctant to die and seeks comfort in the same way that Jesus sought support from his disciples in the Garden of Gethsemane before his death. Just like Jesus, Aslan's purpose is to serve others, obey the will of the Emperor-over-the-Sea (the allegorical equivalent of God) and is prepared to die for others. Aslan is a way of introducing Christianity to children in a memorable way, using an exciting setting, with events and talking animals that will appeal to children. His resurrection is echoed in the way he breathes on the animals turned to stone by the Witch in order to return them to life.

The link with Jesus Christ is never explicitly stressed. Lewis shows us what Aslan/Jesus is like, and how we have to encounter him ourselves and form our own views on him. At the same time, encounters with Aslan/Jesus enable people to discover the truth about themselves and come to terms with their own mistakes.

## MR TUMNUS

Mr Tumnus is a faun, a creature from Greek mythology possessing a mostly human body, but the legs of a goat. He is very important, as the image of a faun in a snowy wood (which is how we are introduced to Mr Tumnus) was the original spark of inspiration that eventually led Lewis to create the world of Narnia. Mr Tumnus meets Lucy on her first visit to Narnia. Although naturally kind, he is overwhelmed and frightened by the Witch's power and agrees to act on her behalf because he does not want to be turned to stone. When he meets Lucy, he finds he cannot do as the Witch requires. He tells Lucy he is a terrible person, but willingly escorts her back towards the Wardrobe and freedom. When the Witch discovers what he has done, his house is ransacked and Mr Tumnus becomes a stone statue in her castle. He is revived by Aslan, and becomes a lifelong friend of Lucy. Mr Tumnus is very keen on tea and toast!

## THE WHITE WITCH

Although her name is Jadis, she is only ever referred to as the White Witch. She also claims to be Queen of Narnia: "She calls herself the Queen of Narnia though she has no right to be Queen at all, and all the Fauns and Dryads and Naiads and Dwarfs and Animals – at least all the good ones – simply hate her" says Lucy (p. 41).

She is evil, cruel and merciless, and is part giant, part Jinn. The White Witch took the throne of Narnia by force and is supported by all kinds of evil creatures. She has placed a spell on Narnia so that it is always winter and never Christmas or spring. This spell can only be broken when the four thrones in Cair Paravel are occupied. She has the right to kill any traitor, and possesses a deadly wand that turns creatures to stone. By playing on Edmund's envy of Peter, and providing him with enchanted food and drink, especially Turkish Delight, she enslaves him to her will.

No direct comparison can be drawn between Jadis and Satan because of the language used to depict her, which is associated with winter and ice – a theme completely at odds with the fire and brimstone typically associated with Satan. It is therefore generally accepted that the White Witch was more likely to be viewed by Lewis as a servant of Satan, rather than Satan himself. Her demise comes in the shape of Aslan, the source of all goodness, reflecting the triumph of good over evil.

## PETER PEVENSIE

Peter is the oldest of the four children. He is 13 years old at the start of *The Lion, the Witch and the Wardrobe* and is accustomed to taking care of his younger siblings. Caring and courageous – qualities that lead to him being named High King by Aslan – Peter is a natural leader. Feeling responsible for his siblings, he seeks advice from Professor Kirke when he is worried that Lucy is telling lies. Once in Narnia, he is immediately willing to acknowledge his mistakes and keen to do the right thing by helping Mr Tumnus. His role as a leader and warrior is further emphasised by the gift of a sword and shield from Father Christmas, weapons which he later uses to protect Susan from the wolf. Aslan places him in charge when Aslan prepares to meet the Witch at the Stone Table. Once crowned, Peter is left to make his own decisions, to mature and grow, developing into a tall, deep-chested man and warrior known as King Peter the Magnificent. He rules for 15 years in Narnia, leaving aged 28. On his return to England he reverts to his original age of 13, as no time has passed in England.

Peter shares the same name as St Peter, the leader of the Apostles. Just like St Peter, Peter takes on leadership roles at the request of Aslan.

## SUSAN PEVENSIE

Susan is the second-oldest of the Pevensie children. She is 12 years old on her arrival in Narnia. Like her siblings, she rules for 15 years, and leaves aged 27, returning to her original age of 12. Susan is a natural beauty, and becomes known as Queen Susan the Gentle. She develops into a tall, gracious woman with black hair that falls almost to her feet, and many suitors begin seeking her hand in marriage. Susan is not a warrior queen; in fact, she dislikes bloodshed and is naturally cautious. This can be seen clearly when they arrive at the house of Mr Tumnus, only to find that the White Witch has captured him. While Peter and Lucy are keen to go to his aid, Susan's reaction is to focus on the danger, and she recommends leaving Narnia immediately. When she meets Father Christmas, she is given a bow and arrow to defend herself, and a magic horn to blow when danger threatens.

## EDMUND PEVENSIE

Edmund is the third-oldest of the Pevensie children. He is nine years old on arrival in Narnia. Like his siblings, he rules for 15 years and leaves aged 24, returning to his original age of nine. At the beginning of the story, Edmund is a nasty, unpleasant, spiteful, mean child who is also greedy, untruthful and envious of Peter. He is told off for continually teasing and making fun of Lucy. He wants to frighten her, and make her feel like she is stupid for believing in Narnia. Edmund is the second of the children to discover Narnia, but his experience is very different to that of Lucy, partly reflecting his character and partly as a means of developing the story-line. He meets the White Witch who recognizes his weaknesses and plays on them. She tells him that she will make him her heir, to rule after her in Narnia, while his siblings will just be princes and princesses in his court. He is given enchanted Turkish Delight which appeals to his greed. On returning through the wardrobe, he refuses to acknowledge he has been to Narnia and says he has just been playing. When Peter seeks the advice of Professor Kirke, Peter is asked which of his two siblings is known to be more truthful - Edmund or Lucy - and is forced to admit that Edmund has more of a tendency towards lying.

Back in Narnia, Edmund rejoins the White Witch and betrays his siblings. Nothing turns out as he had expected. Instead of being a cherished heir to the throne, he becomes a prisoner whose life can be taken by the White Witch as her lawful prey. Rescued by Aslan's forces, he has a long conversation with Aslan, during which he undergoes a transformation. He becomes a loyal supporter of Aslan, showing great courage during the battle with the Witch's followers. Realising that the Witch is winning because of her ability to turn people into stone, he attacks her and focuses on destroying the wand, but sustains a life-threatening wound as a result. His actions ultimately determine the course of the battle. Lucy's cordial is used to save his life. He is never told that Aslan died in his place at the Stone Table. Once reigning in Narnia, he matures into a quiet, grave man who is "great in council and judgment", gaining the name of King Edmund the Just.

## LUCY PEVENSIE

Lucy is the real heroine of the novel. She is the fourth and youngest of the Pevensie children. Lucy is eight years old when she discovers Narnia, and rules for 15 years as Queen until she reaches the age of 23, returning to her original age of eight when she returns to England. She is mocked by Edmund for her belief in Narnia, while Peter and Susan think she is lying or going mad. Her natural character shines throughout the story: she is courageous, cheerful, brave, optimistic, willing to suspend belief, always wanting to help and sees good in people. She is the first to enter Narnia, meeting Tumnus the faun and winning him over to Aslan's side without even knowing she is doing it. On her return to Narnia with her brothers and sister, her immediate reaction upon discovering that Mr Tumnus is in danger is to find a way to save him, even though it might put her own life in danger. Father Christmas gives her a healing cordial, because she is to have no role in the fighting; her role is to heal. Lucy is immediately responsive to Aslan, and accompanies him on his last walk to the Stone Table, giving him what comfort she can. After the battle she uses her cordial to save lives, including that of Edmund. She is much loved by everyone, and is described as "always gay and golden-haired and all the princes in those parts desired her to be their Queen, and her own people called her Queen Lucy the Valiant" (p. 167).

Lucy is the protagonist, the key character from the very beginning of the story, although it eventually becomes clear that Aslan's role is even more crucial than hers. Most of the events of the book are seen through Lucy's eyes.

## MAUGRIM

Maugrim is a Wolf, and chief of the White Witch's secret police. He is evil and follows all her commands. Maugrim is sent to kill all the children, and tracks them to their meeting with Aslan. He chases Susan up a tree, and is killed in battle with Peter.

## DIGORY KIRKE

Digory Kirke is an eccentric, academic, elderly Professor who has opened up his home to four evacuee children: the Pevensies. Professor Kirke is wise and open minded, and knows much more than he lets on. There are hints that Kirke may have been to Narnia himself, hints which are eventually brought to life in a later book, *The Magician's Nephew*, in which it is revealed that he was present at the birth of Narnia. He lives in a big house in the countryside along with his housekeeper, Mrs Macready. When Peter and Susan are worried about Lucy and seek his advice, he adopts a logical attitude, encouraging them to think and make their own decisions based on whether Lucy or Edmund is known to be the most truthful. He helps them to understand that Narnia may well exist.

## MR AND MRS BEAVER

Mr Beaver is Mr Tumnus's friend, and has been warned to watch for Lucy if ever she returns to Narnia. He becomes their guide, providing shelter at his home, where they meet Mrs Beaver, and advises them to seek the help of Aslan. Mr and Mrs Beaver are very kindly, caring creatures who are opposed to the White Witch and are supporters of Aslan. Mrs Beaver is very motherly, caring, good-natured and a good cook.

# ANALYSIS

## CONTEXT AND BACKGROUND

As a children's writer, Lewis has proved incredibly successful. He wanted to write books that he would have enjoyed as a child. He once stated, "I wrote the books I should have liked to read. That has always been my reason for writing. People won't write the books I want, so I have to do it for myself" (Green, 1963: 9). Lewis also believed that the main reason for writing a children's story is that "a children's story is the best art form for something you have to say". (Lewis, 2002: 32)

The ideas came to him in a series of images, beginning with that of the faun, followed by the lamp post and the Queen on a sleigh, and eventually Aslan. The resulting adventure contained elements of Norse and Greek mythology, alongside Christian elements. It was a way in which children could encounter Christ and the central elements of Christianity without having them specifically identified. He wrote "I saw how stories of this kind could steal past a certain inhibition which had paralysed much of my own religion in childhood" (Lewis, 2002: 47). In 1931, long before the book was ready for publication, he wrote a letter addressed to his friend Arthur Greeves saying that he set out his story of Aslan as a retelling of the "actual incarnation, crucifixion and resurrection" (McGrath, 2013).

Similarly, in 1954, Lewis wrote to a fifth-grade class in Maryland saying "Let us suppose that there were a land like Narnia, and that the Son of God, as he became a Man in our world, became a Lion there, and then imagine what would happen" (Dorsett and Lamp Mead, 1996: 45).

Having said that, Lewis was equally happy if his readers just enjoyed the adventure stories and learned some basic morality as a result. Above all, he wanted to use very memorable imagery to encourage people to respond, think and consider some of the deepest questions of life.

## GOOD VS. EVIL

This is the central motif within the story. At the beginning of the novel, evil in the form of a cruel, merciless Queen has triumphed and is holding

Narnia in the throes of winter. There is little joy, hope, happiness or warmth to be found. Aslan – the force of good – comes to break the hold of evil, helped by the arrival of the four Pevensie children who can occupy the vacant thrones at Cair Paravel. The outcome is never completely certain, as the plot introduces new challenges such as Aslan's death, and the White Witch's wand destroying Peter's army. For a time, evil seems to be winning again, but it is ultimately overcome by the forces of good, and Edmund's good deeds.

A lot of the symbolism in the novel is based on the theme of good vs. evil, and reflects the Christian journey towards God. Some of the key messages that this symbolism is intended to convey are the idea that it is easy to fall into temptation and accept evil, as well as the need to constantly make choices that lead towards salvation and the importance of fighting for good.

## THE FALL FROM GRACE AND REDEMPTION

Aslan gives his life for Edmund, which echoes the Christian belief that Jesus gave his life for humanity's sake. Aslan's sacrifice wipes out Edmund's sin and allows Edmund to live. In the same way, Christian doctrine teaches that the death of Jesus served as atonement for the sins of all humanity. By giving his life for Edmund, Aslan destroys the power of the Witch, enabling Narnia to be saved from the power of evil. The Stone Table becomes the equivalent of the Cross. The disappearance of Aslan's body mirrors that of the resurrection, when Jesus's body disappeared from the tomb. Susan, just like Mary Magdalene, asks where Aslan's body has been taken, echoing the Biblical figure of Mary Magdalene, who goes to Jesus' tomb and says "They have taken away my Lord, and I do not know where they have laid him" (John 20:13). Jesus then appears, just as Aslan does to Susan and Lucy. Later, Aslan's breath revives the creatures turned into stone by the Witch's wand, which could be seen as a metaphor for the Christian belief that the Holy Spirit breathes new life into those who follow Jesus.

## GLUTTONY AND ENVY

This is a key theme centred on Edmund and his relationships with Peter and the White Witch. Edmund is envious of his older brother, while gluttony is used to enchant Edmund into entering the Witch's service. He eats Turkish Delight and immediately wants more. He lets himself be controlled by his gluttony and envy, ultimately leading him to join the Witch's side. The consumption of Turkish Delight can be seen as a metaphor for Adam and Eve eating from the Tree of Knowledge, which leads to them being punished and never satisfied.

## UNIVERSAL MORALITY

C. S. Lewis believed in the existence of a common morality to be found throughout humanity, a humanity which he sometimes referred to as a 'natural law'. This entailed a basic standard of behaviour, with an underlying principle which he described as the "foundation of all clear thinking about ourselves and the universe we live in" (Lewis, 2015: 8).

# FURTHER REFLECTION

## SOME QUESTIONS TO THINK ABOUT…

- What makes a good children's story?
- Compare and contrast the key characters.
- How far is *The Lion, the Witch and the Wardrobe* a morality tale?
- Why do you think *The Lion, the Witch and the Wardrobe* has been so popular?
- What is the enduring appeal of this story?
- How far can the story be appreciated as a children's tale rather than an allegory of Christianity?
- To what extent has *The Lion, the Witch and the Wardrobe* influenced the genre of fantasy writing?
- Do the film and TV portrayals of the Pevensie children accurately reflect the book?

*We want to hear from you!*
*Leave a comment on your online library*
*and share your favourite books on social media!*

# FURTHER READING

## REFERENCE EDITION


- Lewis, C. S. (1959) *The Lion, the Witch and the Wardrobe.* London: Penguin.


## REFERENCE STUDIES


- Carpenter, H. (1978) *The Inklings: C. S. Lewis, J. R. R. Tolkien, Charles Williams, and their friends*. London: Harper Collins.
- Dorsett, L. W. and Lamp Mead, M., eds. (1996) *C. S. Lewis: Letters to Children*. New York: Touchstone.
- Green, R. L. (1963) *C.S. Lewis*. London: Bodley Head.
- Lewis, C. S. (2015) *Mere Christianity.* New York: HarperCollins.
- Lewis, C. S. (2002) *On Stories, and Other Essays on Literature.* New York: Harcourt.
- Lewis, C. S. (1955) *Surprised by Joy: The Shape of My Early Life*. London: Geoffrey Bles.
- McGrath, A. (2013) The religious symbolism behind the *Chronicles of Narnia*. *BBC*. [Online]. [Accessed 5 December 2018]. Available from: <http://www.bbc.co.uk/religion/0/24865379>

## ADAPTATIONS

- *The Chronicles of Narnia: The Lion, the Witch and the Wardrobe*. (2005) [Film]. Andrew Adamson. Dir. UK/USA: Walt Disney.
- *The Chronicles of Narnia*. (1988) [TV series]. Marilyn Fox. Dir. UK: BBC.

www.brightsummaries.com

Ebook EAN: 9782808016032

Paperback EAN: 9782808016049

Legal Deposit: D/2018/12603/562



Digital conception by Primento, the digital partner of publishers.

Printed in Great Britain
by Amazon